A Great Day Out

Written by
Helen Orme

Illustrated by
Jacky Rough

Today is a warm, sunny day.
We're going to the seaside!

We will travel by train.
Mum is getting the train tickets.

There are lots of people on the platform. Maybe they are all going to the seaside.

It's just five minutes until the train comes.

I hope it won't be late!

Here comes the train!

Let's sit here. Our bags can go up on the rack.

There goes the whistle!
Off we go!

It's a long way to the seaside.

We've got some games to play and some books to read.

Looking out of the window is fun too. I can see a black horse and some cows.

We can all have a drink from the trolley!

"No, thank you. We don't want anything to eat. We had a lot to eat for breakfast."

Why has the train stopped?
It isn't at a station.

There must be a red light.
The train will be going again soon.

We've arrived at the seaside!
Off we get.

Don't forget to bring the bags!

We can walk to the beach.
It's not far.

We're on the beach!
Quick, let's get into our swimsuits.
I'm going to be first into the sea!